BUGS BUNNY
Rides Again

by JEAN LEWIS
illustrated by JOE MESSERLI

A GOLDEN BOOK • NEW YORK
Western Publishing Company, Inc., Racine, Wisconsin 53404

Bugs Bunny called over the fence to Porky Pig, "What's up, doc?"

"Come and help us clean out the garage," said Porky.

"Oh, I just remembered something I have to do," said Bugs. And he was gone.

"Same old Bugs," said Elmer Fudd, wringing out his mop. "Always running away from work!"

"Who is this?" asked Petunia Pig, dusting off a faded old picture.

"That's Uncle Horatio and Aunt Ima Hogg!" exclaimed Porky. "They won lots of races on their bicycle built for two."

"And here is the bicycle," said Porky, uncovering a rusty two-seater.

"Oh, could we ride it?" begged Petunia.

"Sure," said Porky, "just as soon as I clean it up."

Then Porky found Uncle Horatio's three-wheel bike. He gave it to Elmer as a reward for helping clean out the garage.

Suddenly Petunia had an idea. "Let's celebrate Porky's clean garage by going on a picnic!" she said.

"What a good idea," said Porky. "We can ride the bikes over to Blue Bird Lake!"

While Petunia hurried home to bake a cake,
Porky and Elmer worked on the bikes.
They cleaned and oiled them. Porky pumped
air in the tires while Elmer put a bell on each
bicycle. Then the two went inside to pack a
picnic lunch.

Petunia came back wearing pink pedal pushers and carrying a freshly baked carrot cake.

"Oh, how beautiful!" she exclaimed when she saw the two shiny bikes.

Porky beamed proudly as he tied the picnic basket to the bike.

Then Bugs Bunny came back. "Going someplace?" he asked.

When he heard about the picnic and saw the carrot cake, Bugs was sorry he hadn't helped clean out the garage. Bugs wanted to go on the picnic, too.

Suddenly, he had an idea. "Hey, I'll race all of
you to Blue Bird Lake. Just wait till I rent a
bicycle at Ed's Bike Shop!" And off he went.

"Come on," said Porky. "Let's go without him."

Elmer Fudd shook his head. "No. It's time to teach that lazy, scheming rabbit a lesson," he said. And he ran inside to phone Ed's Bike Shop. He told Ed just what to do.

When Bugs arrived at the bike shop, Ed was ready for him. He showed Bugs a unicycle. "Is this all you've got?" asked Bugs

"This bike was made just for you, Bugs," Ed said. "With your long legs, you'll fly!"

"OK," said Bugs. He took the unicycle and started back to Porky's.

"Here comes Bugs, and he's got the unicycle!" said Elmer.

"I'm ready to race," said Bugs. "That is, if I can get on this crazy bike!" Bugs grabbed the gatepost to keep from falling.

"Tweet!" Elmer blew his whistle and the race was on!

"So long, Bugs!" shouted Elmer as he rode past.

"Bye-bye, Bugs!" yelled Porky and Petunia from their bicycle built for two.

Bugs could barely keep his balance as he wobbled up the road. But he kept pedaling!

Soon Porky, Petunia, and Elmer were enjoying a peaceful picnic at Blue Bird Lake.

"Guess Bugs gave up trying to ride that crazy bike," said Elmer.

Porky took another sandwich while Petunia cut the cake. "I'll save Bugs a piece, just in case he does make it," said Petunia.

Suddenly they heard a scream. There was
Bugs, paws over both eyes, speeding downhill.
"Help! I can't stop this crazy bike!" yelled
Bugs Bunny.

Bugs lifted one paw, spotted the carrot cake, and just at the right moment fell into it headfirst. In no time he had eaten his way out.

"Maybe I lost the race," he said, smacking his lips, "but I won the prize—Petunia's cake!"